For Mali J. ~ M.S.

To Lorenzo and Caterina,
with all my love ~ B.B.

First published in 2017
by Scholastic Children's Books
Euston House, 24 Eversholt Street, London NW1 1DB
a division of Scholastic Ltd
www.scholastic.co.uk
London · New York · Toronto · Sydney · Auckland
Mexico City · New Delhi · Hong Kong

ISBN 978 1407 16483 0
All rights reserved • Printed in Malaysia

3 5 7 9 10 8 6 4 2

The moral rights of Mark Sperring and Barbara Bongini
have been asserted.
Papers used by Scholastic Children's Books are made
from wood grown in sustainable forests.

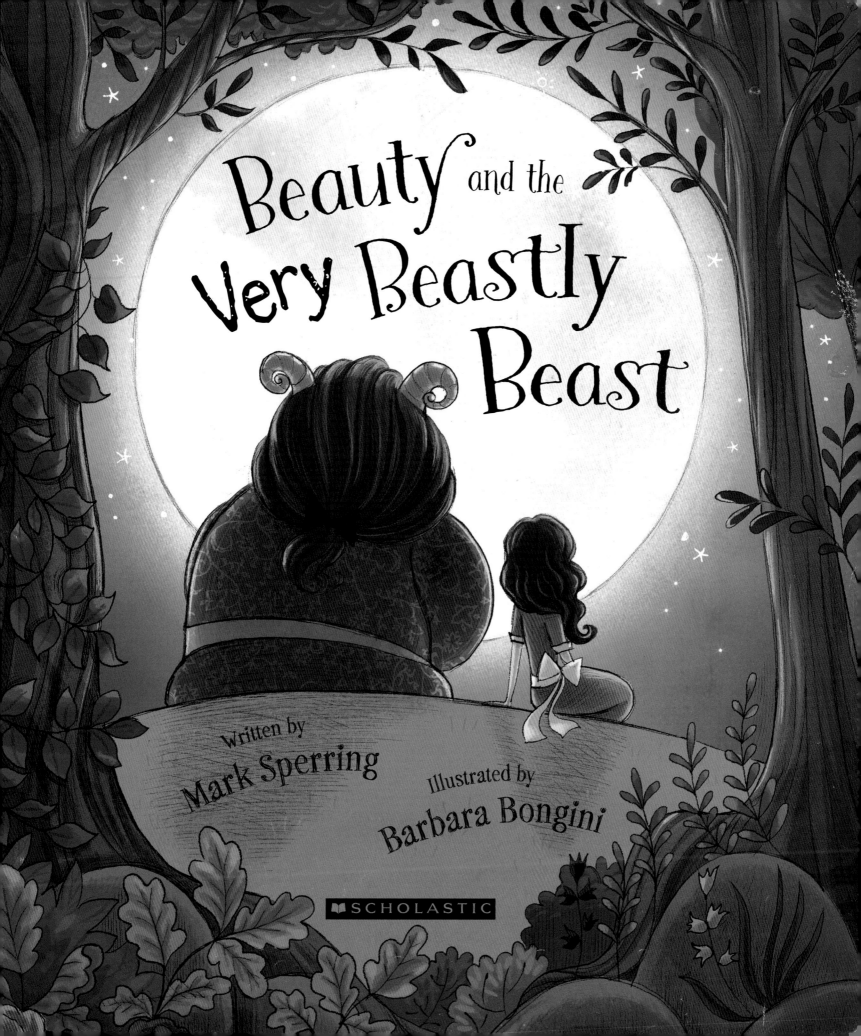

Beauty and the Very Beastly Beast

Written by
Mark Sperring

Illustrated by
Barbara Bongini

SCHOLASTIC

Once upon a time in this cottage RIGHT HERE
lived a girl called Beauty,

her two sisters,
Grace and May,

their darling Popsey,

four hens,

eight ducks,

HISSSS!

...d a rather bad-tempered goose called Irma.

One day, Popsey went on a **trip** into town ...

and promised to bring back **presents** for everyone.

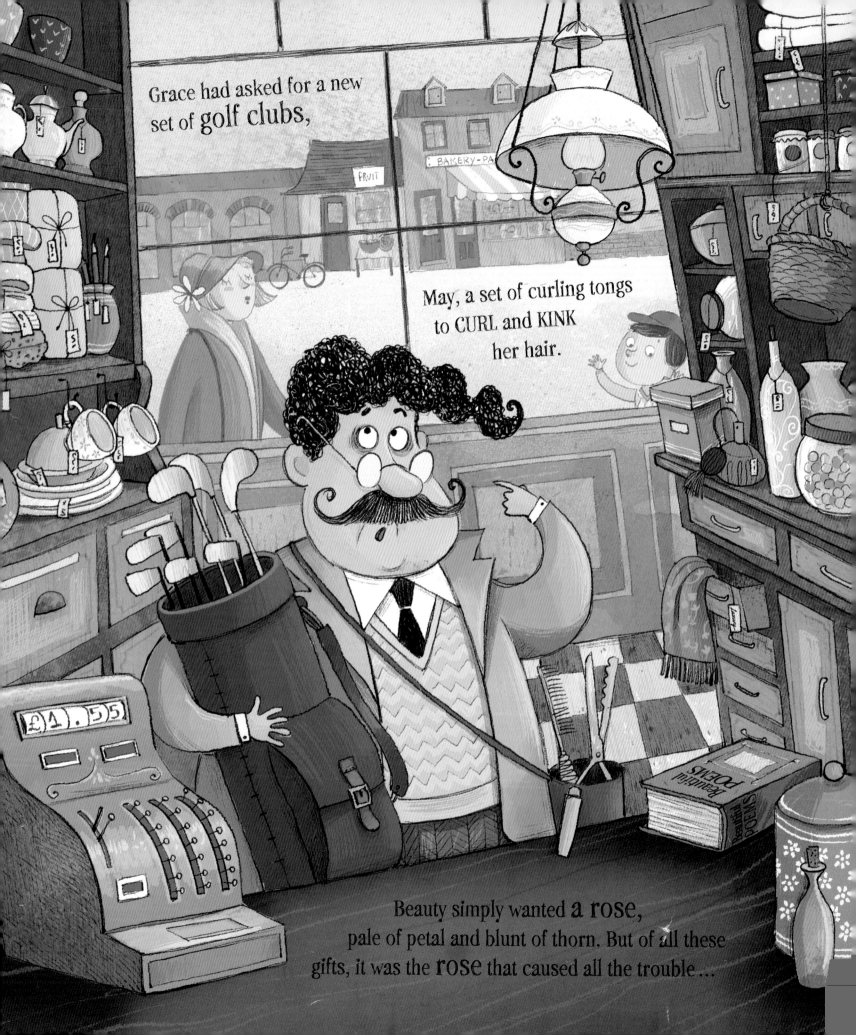

Grace had asked for a new
set of golf clubs,

May, a set of curling tongs
to CURL and KINK
her hair.

£4.55

Beauty simply wanted a rose,
pale of petal and blunt of thorn. But of all these
gifts, it was the rose that caused all the trouble…

Popsey had seen one growing in a LOVELY garden. The problem was the rose was not his to take ...

... and as he reached out to pick it ...

... something TERRIBLE happened.

Popsey hoped that bad-tempered **Irma** would be the first to honk down the path to greet him – but alas that was not to be …

For it was **Beauty** who greeted him at the gate.

"We'll go instead!"

scowled Beauty's sisters when they learnt of her BEASTLY fate.

"Hush!" said Beauty.
"No one can go but me!"

Then, with lots of tears and a
DOUBLE DOLLOP of bravery,
off she went to live with Beast.

When Beauty reached the lovely garden, Beast was busy watering his flowers.

"I was the first living thing to greet my father," she explained, "but could you please find it in your heart to let me go?"

"I'll **think** about it..." said Beast,
And because he was not all bad, he DID think about it...

He thought about it that night over dinner...

Munch!
Gulp!
Slobber!

And he thought about it the next day on a MUDDY morning stroll...

splash!
sploosh!
squelch!

And he thought about it the day **after** that...

And the day after **that**...

Until the days piled up into months...

and whole seasons had blown and blustered by...

But by that time, Beast had totally got used to Beauty being around...

IN FACT...

... he had fallen quite
in love with her!

"Do you think you could ever marry me?"
Beast asked, one moonlit night.

Beauty gazed up at the twinkling stars
and thought for a moment...

And although she had become incredibly fond of the Beast, Beauty was not quite sure.
"I don't know," she sighed.

So Beast gave her a VERY precious gift and said, "Why don't you go home and think about it. And if you don't come back, I'll know your answer..."

Beauty thought about marrying Beast that first morning she reached home ...

But she got so many honks, clucks, quacks and kisses it slipped her mind.

And she thought about it that afternoon...
But she got so caught up in a game of golf it flew clear out of her head.

"Oh, good shot!"

And she thought about it the day **after** that when she and May curled Popsey's hair...

... and in the weeks that followed, when she noticed Beast's rose did not wilt or wither. Yes, for a whole month Beauty did **think** about becoming "Mrs Beast".

But she only **truly** thought about it when she noticed
something **terrible**...

The rose was dead!

"Beast!" cried Beauty.

"I think something **terrible** has happened to Beast!"

Then, without a **word** of goodbye, she tore out of the house leaving a cloud of feathers and flapping wings behind her...

... Beauty rushed to Beast's heartbroken side

and did something

she'd never dreamed of doing...

She kissed him.

And, **as if by magic,** Beast began to change into something rather handsome... **A prince** with **hands** and **feet** instead of paws!

Long ago, a witch had cast a beastly spell on the Prince, because he had not given her a rose...

The spell could only be broken by ...

True love's **kiss!**

"Well," smiled Beauty, "seeing as it's true love, I suppose I shall marry you, although I will miss your charming horns and dashing mane!"

The wedding was a splendid affair.
As for the **bridesmaids**, there were almost too many to count.
There was Grace and May…

…and four hens… and eight ducks.

And, of course, a rather bad-tempered one who
hissed and honked and refused to say "cheese".
But not even a **beastly** bridesmaid could
stop Beauty and her lovely prince living…

... happily ever after!